MW01069506

The Kids in Mrs. Z's Class

Rohan Murthy Has a Plan

The Kids in Mrs. Z's Class

Rohan Murthy Has a Plan

RAJANI LaROCCA

illustrated by **KAT FAJARDO**

Series Coordinated by **KATE MESSNER**

ALGONQUIN YOUNG READERS
WORKMAN PUBLISHING
NEW YORK

Copyright © 2024 by Rajani LaRocca
Illustrations © 2024 by Kat Fajardo
Cover art color and interior shading by Pablo A. Castro
Kraft paper texture © klyaksun/Shutterstock
Paw print © pingebat/Shutterstock

Algonquin Young Readers
Workman Publishing
Hachette Book Group, Inc.
1290 Avenue of the Americas
New York, NY 10104
workman.com

Algonquin Young Readers is an imprint of Workman Publishing, a division of Hachette Book Group, Inc. The Workman name and logo are registered trademarks of Hachette Book Group, Inc.

Design by Neil Swaab

The publisher is not responsible for websites (or their content) that are not owned by the publisher.

Workman books may be purchased in bulk for business, educational, or promotional use. For information, please contact your local bookseller or the Hachette Book Group Special Markets Department at special.markets@hbgusa.com.

Library of Congress Cataloging-in-Publication Data is available.
ISBN 978-1-5235-2658-1 (hardcover)
ISBN 978-1-5235-2659-8 (paperback)
First Edition May 2024 LSC-C
Printed in the USA on responsibly sourced paper.

10 9 8 7 6 5 4 3 2 1

For all the kids who want to make a difference

MEET The Kids in Mrs. Z's Class

Adam

Ayana

Carlota

Emma

Poppy

Rohan

Ruthie

Sebastian

Steven

Chapter 1

A Very Valued Visitor

Rohan Murthy's class was starting the school day outside.

"I wonder what's going on?" Rohan whispered to his best friend, Adam.

"I don't know, but it's great to be out in the sun instead of stuck in our classroom," Adam said.

Rohan kicked at the rectangular patch of bare dirt. They were behind the school, not far from the playground and a small grove of trees.

"So, third graders, this is a place where we'll be doing some learning this fall and in the spring. What do you think will go here?" Mrs. Z asked.

"It's small for a soccer field," Rohan said. "Maybe a playground?"

"We already have that. How about a water park?" Ayana asked.

"No one has a water park at school," said Sebastian.

"We could plant something," Steven said.

"Exactly. This is the space for our new Curiosity Academy garden," Mrs. Z said. "We'll need help from the whole school community. We're going to plant bulbs this fall, sprout seeds indoors in the late winter, and start our outside garden in the spring. We'll need ideas about what to plant, and lots of hands for digging and weeding."

"We could plant flowers," Fia said.

"And vegetables," Emma said.

"Maybe even a tree," Rohan said. "Every new tree helps the planet."

"That would be pretty expensive," Memo said.

"We'll also need help raising money for all our garden plans, so think about ideas for that, too," Mrs. Z said.

I'd love to help raise money for the garden, Rohan thought. *We should make it the most awesome garden possible!*

Back inside, Rohan looked at the board.

The Daily Scribble
for Monday, September 16

what are you looking forward to this week?

Rohan smiled and wrote:

I'm looking forward to thinking more about the school garden. But first, I'm excited about our Valued Visitor this morning!

Rohan drew a picture of a woman with curly hair and glasses and her hands on her hips like a superhero. Then he glanced at his mom talking with Mrs. Z, and his chest filled with pride.

Mrs. Z said, "I'm thrilled to introduce our first Valued Visitor of the year—Rohan's mom, Shilpa Murthy. Please join me in giving her a very warm third-grade welcome!"

Everyone in the class clapped for Mom. Rohan clapped the loudest. Even Honey, the class guinea pig, seemed excited, squeaking and hopping around in her cage.

"Good morning, third graders!" Mom said. "I'm so thrilled to visit you. Today, I'm going to tell you about starting a new business. Please feel free to take notes or draw."

Rohan grinned as he turned the page in his notebook.

"As a kid, I loved to draw. I doodled in the margins of my notebooks all the time." As Mom talked, she drew a notebook filled with squiggles on the board.

Rohan looked down at his own doodle-filled notebook. He loved that he shared this with his mom. Drawing was how they both got some of their best ideas.

"Later, I went to art school and learned to do all kinds of art," Mom continued, "but drawings and cartoons were always my favorites. After I finished school, I worked at a bunch of different jobs. Then one day, a friend saw one of my drawings and asked me to make one for her, and I realized I could combine the things I love most: making art and making people happy. Customers send me photographs, and I make special drawings of people they love." She drew a portrait of a person smiling. "I needed to learn how to make art quickly, and how to find customers, but now I run a successful business."

Mom clasped her hands. "So with that in mind, I want to talk to you about starting your own businesses. First, you need an idea. Who has an idea for a business?"

Lots of kids raised their hands. Mom called on Poppy.

"I'd like to start a baking business," Poppy said. Rohan noticed that her earrings looked like little cupcakes. So cool!

"Great," Mom said. She wrote "Idea: Baking

Business" on the board and drew a little cupcake next to it. "In order to be successful, it's important to plan out how your business will work. First, try to identify a need in the community. Why would people need Poppy's business?" Mom asked. She wrote "Community Needs" on the board.

"People always need fun treats for celebrations," Emma said.

"And everyone likes cupcakes and cookies," Memo said.

"Excellent," Mom said. "Another thing to think about is how your business will be different from others that do similar things. For example, I draw cartoon images of people in my unique style."

"I like to combine interesting flavors when I bake," Poppy said. "Like blueberry and rose, or green tea and white chocolate."

"And the decorations could be special, depending on what someone is celebrating," Lucy said.

"That would definitely make this business unique," Mom said as she wrote on the board. "Now, third-grade friends, for the next section of our business plan: What kinds of things would Poppy need for her bakery?"

"Flour," said Olive.

"Butter," said Synclaire. "And sugar."

"Decorations," said Fia.

"And special flavorings," Theo said.

"How about boxes and signs?" asked Ayana.

"Great ideas!" Mom wrote their suggestions on the board along with little doodles of each item. "Next, let's think about finding customers. Where do you think Poppy might sell her treats?"

"At a school bake sale," Wyatt suggested.

"Outside, in her neighborhood," Thunder said.

Rohan stuck his hand high in the air. "At the Peppermint Falls Autumn Festival!"

The Autumn Festival was coming up in a couple of weeks on the banks of Lake Bluewater. There would be food—hot dogs and ice cream and cotton candy. There would be music—even a banjo band! And there would be lots of people enjoying themselves outside. It was one of Rohan's favorite things about living in Peppermint Falls.

"We've listed all these things in our business plan—our idea, what makes this idea unique, why it's needed in the community, what items we would require, and where we might get customers," Mom said. "The last thing to consider is *why* you want to create this business.

Why would it make you happy, Poppy?" she asked.

"I love baking," Poppy said. "It's my favorite thing to do."

Theo raised his hand. "And cookies and cupcakes make other people happy."

"You could use the money to buy toys," said Lucy.

"Or you could use the money to help someone else or a cause you believe in," Carlota said.

That's it! Rohan's mind whirled and swirled. Rohan cared about both the school community and the planet, and the school garden would be good for both. He thought and thought as he doodled on his paper.

By the time Mom was finished and the whole class clapped again, Rohan had decided he wanted to start a business to help raise money for the school garden. He could get lots of customers at the Autumn Festival, and then keep the business going all year long.

Rohan had a plan. Now he just needed an idea.

Chapter 2
Around the Lake

That evening, Rohan waited in his driveway for the rest of his family. They were going to ride bikes around Lake Bluewater. It was taking his little sister, Kavya, forever to get her helmet on because she wanted to do it without any help.

He spotted his friend Emma pushing a stroller down the sidewalk. "Hi, Emma!" he called.

"Hi, Rohan," said Emma with a smile. She was wearing a pink-and-purple T-shirt that said, SCIENCE: IT'S LIKE MAGIC, BUT REAL. And she wasn't pushing around a little brother or sister—it was her little brown dog!

"I never asked why you put your dog in a stroller," Rohan said.

"Bongo's getting older," Emma said. "So he can't walk very far anymore. But he needs fresh air, so I take him out in the stroller."

"What if you're busy?" Rohan asked. "You're on a cheerleading team, right?"

"Yeah, but Bongo needs to go out twice a day, every day, so if I don't take him, my mom or dad has to do it," Emma said. "My sisters are too little."

"Hmm." An idea sparked in Rohan's head.

"Want to pet him?" Emma asked.

Rohan looked at Bongo. He had big brown eyes, a tongue that stuck out a little, and a row of tiny, sharp teeth. "No thanks," he said. "I'll see you tomorrow at school."

"Okay. Bye, Rohan." Emma waved as she continued down the sidewalk.

Mom, Dad, and Kavya finally came out of the garage on their bikes. Rohan looked both ways and led his family across Bluebird Lane, followed by Dad, then Kavya, then Mom.

The lake sparkled with late-afternoon sunlight, and the fresh breeze felt good on Rohan's face as they sped along. Kavya said, "I want to be in front. But I'm scared of going too fast!"

Rohan let his sister take the lead. "Go ahead, Kavya," he said. "Don't be scared. You don't need to go faster than you want to."

Kavya squealed and her hair blew from under her helmet as she pedaled fast in front of him.

"Great job, Kavya," Dad called from behind him. "Make sure you watch out for walkers."

Rohan slowed so that he wouldn't get in front of Kavya. "On your left," he called as they passed an older man and woman walking a little dog with floppy ears and a wagging curly tail.

Rohan's idea sparked a little brighter.

As he rode around the lake with his family, Rohan counted how many people were out walking their dogs: *fifteen*!

He saw small dogs, medium-sized dogs, and large dogs. Some dogs walked behind their owners, stopping to sniff along the path.

Some raced in front, pulling their people along. Everyone seemed to be having a great time.

How hard can it be to walk a dog? Rohan thought.

Rohan and his family finished their circuit of the lake and took a break to drink some water.

"That was fun," Kavya said. "I got to be leader the whole time!"

"You did a great job," Mom said.

Dad laid a hand on Rohan's shoulder. "Thanks for giving your sister the chance to lead today," he whispered.

"No problem," Rohan whispered back with a smile. It was worth having time to think about his big idea.

"Watch out!" someone called.

The biggest dog Rohan had ever seen was

barreling toward them! It was pulling a teenage girl behind it. The dog had fluffy brown-and-white fur and a huge brown nose. Drool dripped from its open mouth, which was filled with huge, pointy teeth. Rohan froze.

"Tiny! Stop it!" called the girl. She pulled on the dog's leash and finally got the dog to stop. "Sit!" she said.

The dog sat right in front of Kavya.

"Oh, can I pet the doggy?" Kavya asked.

"Sure," said the girl. "I'm Amanda, and this is Tiny. He's very friendly. He's just a puppy, so he sometimes wants to run too fast."

That enormous dog was a *puppy*? Rohan couldn't imagine how big it would be when it was full-grown.

"Let him sniff your hand, like this," Mom said, showing Kavya what to do.

Kavya reached out, and Tiny sniffed her hand. "Oh! Tiny kissed me," she said, giggling. She petted the dog's enormous head. "Good doggy."

"Do you have to walk Tiny every day?" Rohan asked while Mom and Dad petted the dog, too.

"Three or four times a day," said Amanda. She laughed. "He has a lot of energy."

"I'll bet," Dad said. "Want to pet him, Rohan?"

Rohan rubbed the base of his thumb. "You sure it's safe?" he asked Amanda.

"Definitely," she said.

Rohan held out his hand for the dog to sniff. He closed his eyes as the huge mouth came close.

The dog touched Rohan's hand with its wet nose, and Rohan opened an eye. He reached out his finger and brushed Tiny's head before drawing his hand back again.

That wasn't that hard.

Now Rohan knew how he could raise money for the school garden.

Chapter 3
The Plan Comes Together

The next day, Rohan talked to Adam at their lockers before class. Adam and Rohan had been at their previous school together since kindergarten, and Rohan was glad they were both at Curiosity Academy.

"What did you do yesterday after school?" Rohan asked.

"I got to play my flight simulator game for half an hour. It was awesome," Adam said. "How about you?"

"I went bike riding with my family, and I got a new idea," Rohan said.

Adam smiled. "You always have new ideas."

"I want to raise money for the school garden by starting a dog-walking business!"

Adam raised his eyebrows. "Since when do you like dogs?"

"I like dogs okay," Rohan said. "But more importantly, there are lots and lots of people who *really* like them. And dogs need to be walked every day. Sometimes more than once a day. Remember what my mom said, that a business should meet a need in the community? I'd help my customers *and* the school garden."

"Why stop at dogs?" Adam asked. "Maybe people with other pets need help, too. Like hamsters. And snakes. And cats."

"That's a great idea," Rohan said. "Maybe not cats, though."

"What's wrong with cats?" Adam asked.

"They don't need to be walked, that's all."

"Neither do hamsters or snakes," Adam reminded him.

Rohan grinned. "Thank goodness!"

The two friends went inside the classroom.

"Good morning, Rohan. Good morning, Adam," Mrs. Z said.

"Good morning, Mrs. Z," Rohan said. "Are you wearing radish earrings?"

"Beets," said Mrs. Z. "One of my favorite veggies."

"Maybe we could plant some in the school garden," Rohan said.

"What a lovely idea," said Mrs. Z.

Rohan sat down and looked at the board.

The Daily Scribble
for Tuesday, September 17

what did you learn from our valued visitor yesterday?

I learned that when you start a business, you should try to make yourself and other people happy.

I learned it's not enough to just have a good idea—you also need a plan.

I didn't learn that my mom was awesome.
I already knew that. ☺

Next, the class did some math problems. After Rohan finished, he doodled in the margins of his notebook, sketching different kinds of dogs. He drew hamsters and snakes. He even added a little sketch of Honey the guinea pig chewing some hay.

"Those are really good drawings," Poppy said.

"Thanks," Rohan said. "I really like your bakery idea. I hope you do it. And I can help if you'd like me to make posters."

Poppy smiled.

When Rohan got home that afternoon, he went to the computer in the kitchen.

"What are you doing?" Kavya asked.

"I'm writing a business plan," Rohan said proudly. "Mom taught us how to make one on Valued Visitor Day."

"Ooh, can I help?" Kavya asked. "Pinky Pig wants to help, too." She held up her stuffed pig.

"This is big-kid work," Rohan said. "Third grade, not first grade."

"No fair," Kavya said, frowning and crossing her arms.

Rohan thought quickly before she could call for Mom. "Maybe you could help decorate the pages after I'm done?"

"Yes!" Kavya said. "I'll go get some glitter!" She ran up the stairs to her room.

Rohan was pleased with himself. He typed up his business plan.

Business Plan for Rohan's Pet Care Business

What: I would get clients who need help caring for their pets—walking, feeding, and playing

Community Need: There are a lot of pet owners who could use help

How My Business Is Different:

- Pet sitting with a smile!
- I wouldn't charge as much money as other people
- I'm willing to consider unusual animals, like hamsters and snakes

Things I Need:

- Me!
- All leashes, food, and other supplies come from the pet owners
- Paper, markers, and pens to advertise

Where I Would Find Customers:

- All of Peppermint Falls! At least, the parts I can get to by bike

- I could put up posters in our neighborhood, at school, and in the community center
- Have a table at the Autumn Festival

Why This Makes Me Happy:
- Helpful to older people and busy people with pets
- Even more time outside
- Raise money for Curiosity Academy's new school garden

Rohan printed the plan and started drawing various pets in the margins.

Then Kavya reappeared with a glue stick and glitter. "Ooh, I love your drawings! Wait, you want to take care of pets? But you don't like animals."

"Of course I like animals," Rohan said. "Everyone does."

"But you don't want to touch them," Kavya said.

Rohan shook his head. "I don't need to touch them to take care of them."

Kavya scrunched her face. "I kind of think you do," she said as she patted Pinky Pig.

Rohan blew out a breath. "Do you want to help or not?"

"I want to help," Kavya said. She looked at the paper again. "Hamsters and snakes?"

Rohan nodded. "People have all kinds of pets, not just dogs."

Kavya shrugged. "Let's decorate." She closed her eyes. "First you have to *feel* like a pet."

"What are you talking about?" Rohan asked.

"Imagine you're a dog," Kavya said.

"Kavya . . ."

"Just close your eyes and imagine you're a dog," Kavya said.

"Fine." Rohan closed his eyes.

"What do you want, Rohan the dog?" Kavya asked.

"More snacks? More toys? More time outside?" Rohan replied.

"Excellent. You can draw those on your plan."

"Good idea." Rohan added a ball, a squeaky toy, and some dog bones to his business plan. He drew a piece of broccoli for a hamster, and a couple of crickets for a snake. "There," Rohan said.

"Now it's time for the final touch," Kavya said. She smeared glue and sprinkled glitter all over Rohan's business plan.

Rohan was ready. It was time to share his plan with his parents.

Chapter 4

A Presentation and a Problem

Rohan thought about how Shark Codely from his favorite cartoon always said, "Dress for success!" After dinner, he went upstairs to put on the kurta-pyjama he had worn to Mom's cousin's wedding. When he glanced in the mirror, he thought he looked like someone who was smart, confident, and successful.

He looked again. What was on his collar?

Glitter.

He tried to brush it off, but it stayed stuck.

Oh, well. He went downstairs with his business plan.

Mom and Dad were in the living room.

"I have something to show you," Rohan said.

"What's going on, buddy?" Dad asked.

"And why are you all dressed up?" Mom said.

"You look fancy," Kavya said, curling up on the sofa with Pinky Pig.

"I'd like to present a business plan," Rohan said. "Just like Mom taught us in school yesterday."

Mom and Dad looked at each other and smiled.

"I'd like to start a pet care business," Rohan said. "I'll make sure to finish my schoolwork first, and I'll only go places I can reach by bike. I'd be helping busy pet owners but also raising money for the new school garden. We might even plant a tree!"

He talked through what he needed and how the business would make him happy. At the end of his presentation, Mom, Dad, and Kavya all clapped. Kavya even took a bow.

"Great job," Mom said.

"Very impressive," Dad said. "And I love that you want to raise money for a very worthy cause." Dad was an environmental lawyer, and he cared a lot about green spaces for people and animals.

"And you're very sparkly," Kavya added.

"Great! So I can do it?" Rohan asked.

Mom and Dad glanced at each other again.

"There's just one problem," Mom said.

"And it's a big one," Dad said.

What? Rohan had thought of everything.

"You don't have any experience with animal care," Mom said. "And that's important, because you'd be in charge of these animals. They'd depend on you. Their owners would depend on you, too."

"You don't even really like to touch animals," Dad said.

"See?" said Kavya. "I told you!"

Rohan shook his head. "I can do it! I know I can."

"You have to think things through," Mom said. "Remember what happened with your limeade stand last year?"

Rohan's face got hot. "Well, I had a lot of customers."

"Yes, but you ran out of sugar," Dad said. "So you served straight lime juice."

Kavya puckered her mouth. "It was *really* sour."

"People still enjoyed it, kind of," Rohan said.

"And then you ran out of limes. But your friends had already brought a lot of customers to the stand."

"They still got to drink water," Rohan said.

"I'm sorry, sweetie," Mom said. "But we can't say yes until you can prove to us that you can take care of animals first."

"But I wanted to have a table at the Autumn Festival in two weeks," Rohan said.

"If you think of another way to try this out, then tell us," Mom said.

"But until then, we have to say no," Dad said.

Rohan trudged upstairs with a heavy feeling

in his chest. He took off his nice clothes and got ready for bed. He knew his plan was great. He just had to find a way to convince his parents.

Then he remembered he needed to practice violin. His lesson was the next day, and he'd been so excited about his new idea that he hadn't practiced as much as he wanted to.

The violin sounded extra scratchy.

Next, he took out his recorder and tried "Mary Had a Little Lamb." It didn't sound at all like when Mrs. Berry had played it during music class.

"What are you doing? You're hurting my ears," Kavya said as she came into the room.

"I'm practicing the recorder," Rohan said. "If it hurts your ears, you can stay out of my room."

"My ears don't hurt when you're not playing."

"Kavya—"

"I just wanted to tell you I'm sorry Mom and Dad don't agree with your business idea," she said. "Here. You can sleep with Pinky tonight." She put the pig on Rohan's bed.

"Thanks. Good night," Rohan said.

Rohan thought and thought as he drifted off to sleep. He thought some more over breakfast the next morning, and while talking to Adam on the bus. Maybe he could ask Emma to bring Bongo over some afternoon. Or he could go to the park and ask to walk different dogs. Maybe someone had a snake he could borrow.

Then Mrs. Z said something that changed everything.

"I have an exciting announcement," Mrs. Z said at the beginning of class on Wednesday. "This weekend will be the first time that

Honey the guinea pig will be going home with someone from the class. It's a big responsibility: The student will need to give Honey food and water. They will need to keep her cage clean. They'll need to play with her and make sure she is happy. If you'd like to take Honey home with you, please sign up here and bring this information sheet home to your parents."

This was perfect!

Rohan needed to prove to his parents that he could take care of a pet.

And Honey needed a home for the weekend.

He raced to the sign-up sheet and put his name first.

Chapter 5
That Cat

That afternoon, Rohan ran home from the bus stop with Kavya. "Mom," he called. "Dad!"

"Hello, kids," Mom said as she gave them both a hug.

"What's all the excitement about?" Dad came into the kitchen from his home office.

"Rohan has an idea!" Kavya said, jumping up and down.

Rohan reached into his backpack and pulled out the piece of paper that Mrs. Z had given him. "Honey the guinea pig needs a home for the weekend, so I signed up to take her."

He waited for a few minutes while Mom and Dad read the information sheet.

"We don't have plans to go anywhere this weekend," Mom said. "We can help if you need groceries for Honey. You can make us a list."

Rohan nodded. "And I'll take care of everything else to make sure Honey is happy and healthy. If I can do this, will you let me start my pet care business?"

"We'll consider it," Dad said.

"Hooray!" Kavya jumped up and down again, and this time Rohan joined her.

Mom smiled. "Now, who wants a snack?"

"Do I smell pakoras?" Dad asked. Pakoras were yummy savory fritters, and the whole family loved them.

They all ate some pakoras and fruit. Mom and Dad had tea, and Rohan and Kavya drank milk.

Soon, it was time for Rohan's violin lesson with Mrs. Steele next door.

"Can you bring some of these pakoras to Mrs. Steele?" Mom asked.

"Sure," Rohan said.

"Maybe you can ask her if she needs any help with her cat," Dad added.

Rohan froze.

"You okay, Rohan?" Kavya asked.

"Of course," he said.

Rohan grabbed his violin case and sheet music from his room. Then he took the bag with the pakoras and went next door to Mrs. Steele's house. As he walked up the front steps, he saw a small gray animal with bright yellow eyes watching him from the front window.

It was Mrs. Steele's cat, Luna.

Rohan swallowed as he rang the doorbell.

Mrs. Steele had short gray hair and big blue eyes. "Ready for your lesson, Rohan?"

"Yes, Mrs. Steele. Also, Mom made pakoras and thought you might like some." Rohan handed her the bag. "There's mint chutney in there, too."

"How lovely. Thank you," Mrs. Steele said. Her glasses moved up her nose as she smiled.

Luna had come over from the window and was weaving in and around Mrs. Steele's legs. Rohan couldn't stop staring at her. He rubbed the base of his thumb.

"Rohan? Is everything all right?" Mrs. Steele asked.

He blinked. "Yes. Sorry."

"Come with me and let's start your lesson."

Rohan followed Mrs. Steele into her living

room. He opened his violin case, and Luna took off into another room.

"She doesn't enjoy violin as much as we do," Mrs. Steele said.

Rohan nodded. He played the violin piece he'd been working on for the week, called "Lightly Row."

"Good job, Rohan," Mrs. Steele said at the end of the lesson. "A little more practice during the week might help, though. What do you think?"

"Yes, I can practice more," Rohan said. He'd have to add it to schoolwork, recorder practice, reading, and getting flyers and posters ready for his pet care business.

"Thank you for the snacks," she said as they walked to the front door. "Would you like to stay and have some with me? I have cookies, too."

Luna was back, sitting next to Mrs. Steele's foot and glaring at Rohan.

"I'm full. Thank you, though," Rohan said.

"All right then, I'll see you next week," Mrs. Steele said. She waved as Rohan walked back toward his house.

"Want to draw something?" Kavya asked as he came in the door.

"Maybe later," Rohan said.

He ran up to his room and sat on his bed. He rubbed his thumb again. It didn't hurt. There were no bite marks on it.

Not like the time he went to Mrs. Steele's house last year. He had finished his lesson, and Luna had come over and brushed against his leg. When he had reached out to pet her, she'd sunk her teeth into his thumb in a flash.

He had gone to the bathroom and washed his hands. She hadn't even broken the skin.

But it had *hurt*. He hadn't thought Luna would hurt him. Or that she had so many teeth.

Rohan hadn't told anyone—he was too embarrassed. And maybe a little scared. Luna had always seemed so friendly.

He took a deep breath and looked at the instruction sheet for bringing Honey home.

Honey was a guinea pig, not a cat. She wasn't going to be scary at all.

Rohan was sure of it.

Almost.

Chapter 6
Plans and More Plans

Before school the next day, Kavya practiced her Bharatanatyam dance steps while Rohan played his recorder in the kitchen.

Stomp, stomp, stomp-stomp-stomp went Kavya's feet.

"Do you have to do that right now?" Rohan asked.

"I have to practice for my dance performance," Kavya said. "I'm scared I'm going to mess up."

"Well, I have to practice recorder for music class, and you're making me mess up." Rohan started playing again.

"What song is that?" Mom asked.

"'Mary Had a Little Lamb,'" Rohan said.

"Are you sure?" Dad asked.

"Of course I am!"

"Pinky says that makes her ears hurt," Kavya said.

Stomp-stomp-stomp-stomp, stomp, stomp.

Rohan played louder.

"It sounds like the lamb might be in pain," Kavya said.

"Time for the bus, kids," Dad said loudly.

After announcements, Mrs. Z asked the class how third grade was going so far.

"It's fun," Rohan said.

"Yes," Ruthie said. "It's great to be in a new school."

"That's good to hear," Mrs. Z said. "But sometimes, even when things are exciting, we can have some things that we're worried about, and that's okay. So here is today's Daily Scribble."

Mrs. Z wrote on the board:

what are you nervous or scared about right now?

Rohan frowned at his notebook. Kavya was a little kid. She had plenty of things that made her scared. But he was a big brother, and he had a plan for everything. He wrote:

I'm not nervous about anything.

I'm excited about having Honey at our house this weekend and then starting a new business!

At lunchtime, Rohan talked to his friends about his pet care idea.

"That's so cool," Emma said. "Taking care of pets is fun."

"And it's awesome that you want to help raise money for the school garden," Mars said.

"I can tell folks in my neighborhood. Are you making flyers?" Synclaire asked.

"Yes, and posters," Rohan said. "I'm bringing some to the Autumn Festival."

"I can help you," Adam said.

"Me too," Olive added.

Poppy tapped Rohan on the arm. "If you like, I can bring some pet-themed cookies to the festival. That might help you get some customers," she said.

"That would be fantastic, Poppy." Rohan grinned.

During free time in the afternoon, Mrs. Z told Rohan how to take care of Honey. Rohan took notes and doodled in his notebook.

"I'll send hay, paper bedding, and food pellets home with you," Mrs. Z said. "And you can give her fresh veggies and fruit like we do here in our classroom."

Rohan nodded. He made a list of foods for Mom and Dad to get from the grocery store: lettuce, carrots, celery, strawberries.

"You'll need to clean her cage and throw away her droppings each day," Mrs. Z said.

Rohan wrinkled his nose and nodded again.

"And you'll need to play with her," Mrs. Z said with a smile. "She's used to having lots of people around."

Many of Rohan's classmates liked to pet Honey, and even pick her up and cuddle her. Rohan wasn't interested in doing either, but he could try.

Rohan nodded. "Thanks for putting your trust in me, Mrs. Z." He drew a quick sketch of Honey smiling.

"Thanks for taking this responsibility so seriously, Rohan," Mrs. Z said. "I appreciate it, and so will Honey. Animals can't talk like we do, but they find ways of letting us know how they feel."

Rohan went to Honey's cage. He did like animals. He reminded himself that Honey was a guinea pig, not a cat. A very cute, friendly guinea pig.

He took a deep breath.

He stuck a finger inside Honey's cage to pet her fluffy fur.

"Don't stick your fingers inside the cage," Mrs. Z reminded him. "Honey sometimes thinks they look like carrots and tries to nibble them."

Rohan snapped his hand back.

Chapter 7
Honey's Homecoming

The Daily Scribble
for Friday, September 20

What fun plans do you have for this weekend?

I'm taking care of Honey at my house this weekend. We're ready with veggies and fruit. I'm keeping her in my room so she won't be lonely. Once I've had a great weekend with Honey, I can start my pet care business!

Emma raised her hand. "Guess what tomorrow is? It's National Elephant Appreciation Day! I'm going to try to learn more about our school mascot this weekend."

"Great idea," Rohan said as he high-fived his friend.

"What are you going to call your business?" Emma asked Rohan at lunch. "It should be something snappy."

"How about Rohan's Rare Pet Care?" Adam asked.

"That makes it sound like he only takes care of weird pets, like tarantulas," said Sebastian.

Rohan gulped. "I mainly want to take care of regular pets."

"Rohan's Ready to Pet?" Poppy suggested.

"Um . . . ," Rohan started.

"How about Rohan's Cuddly Pet Care?" Ayana asked.

"I'm not going to do that much cuddling," Rohan said. "I think I'm going to just call it Rohan's Pet Care."

"Fine, but it won't stand out that much," Sebastian said.

"But it will fit pretty easily on a poster," Emma noted.

Poppy handed out cookies at the end of lunch. "What do you think?" she asked.

The cookies were round and decorated with dog and cat faces.

"These are adorable!" Ayana said.

"Ooh, mine has a sweet cat with yellow eyes," Emma said.

Rohan flinched.

"This one's for you," Poppy said, handing a special cookie to Rohan.

"Is that Honey?" Rohan asked.

Poppy nodded. "I hope you have fun with her."

"You ready for this weekend?" Adam asked.

"It shouldn't be that hard," Rohan said.

That afternoon, Mom picked up Rohan and Kavya at school so they could bring Honey home together. Mrs. Z handed Mom a bag of supplies, and Rohan carried Honey's cage to the car. He put her cage on the back seat between him and Kavya.

"Oh, she's so cute!" Kavya cried. "Honey, I can't wait for you to meet Pinky Pig!"

"Pinky Pig isn't a real animal," Rohan said.

"She's about Honey's size, though," Kavya said. "They could be friends."

Rohan rolled his eyes. "They can't be friends, because *Pinky Pig isn't actually alive.*"

"You don't understand anything about friendship," Kavya said.

When they got home, Mom told Kavya to get ready to go to her dance class.

"But I want to play with Honey!" Kavya said.

"You can play with her when we return."

"Fine," Kavya said. She turned to Rohan. "Don't have too much fun without me, okay?"

"I'll try," Rohan said.

"I've got a few things to finish up in my office," Dad said. "Just come get me if you need anything, okay?"

"Thanks, Dad. I'll get Honey set up in my room, and then I need to practice violin and recorder."

"Maybe you should practice them in your room," Dad said. "I have to be on a call."

"And you wouldn't want the sound of Mary's crying lamb in the background," said Kavya.

"You know it's 'Mary Had a Little Lamb,' Kavya," Rohan said. He gritted his teeth.

"If you say so. Well, I've got to go to dance practice," Kavya said. And she followed Mom into the garage.

Rohan brought Honey up to his room. He put the cage on his desk, where she could look out the window to his backyard. He filled her water bottle from the bathroom sink and made sure she had plenty of hay in the hay rack in her cage.

"There," Rohan said. "Now you should be comfortable and happy, Honey."

He thought about petting her, but then he remembered what Mrs. Z said. He didn't want his finger nibbled.

Honey wasn't hopping around the cage. She wasn't chirping. She was smooshed all the way in a corner, quivering.

Rohan had to make Honey happy. Otherwise, he'd never convince Mom and Dad that he could start his pet care business. But he didn't know what to do. He stared at her for a while, but she didn't leave the corner.

Rohan got out his notebook and made sketches of Honey. Some were of her hanging out in her corner, but others were of Honey jumping around her cage like she did at school. He drew Honey munching on a piece of strawberry, smiling.

He showed Honey his pictures.

She didn't stop quivering.

"Come on, Honey. It's all right. Be happy."

But Honey didn't look happy.

"Guess I'll practice my violin," Rohan said. He opened the case and put the sheet music on his bed, then started to play "Lightly Row."

He played it through once, and then noticed a funny noise. A squeaking.

He turned toward Honey's cage. Did she like his violin playing?

Honey was still quivering in the corner of her cage. Maybe she was happy while the music was playing? Rohan lifted his bow and started playing again.

Honey squealed. She started scrambling up the wire of the cage.

She was trying to escape.

"Looks like you enjoy the violin as much as Kavya does," Rohan said.

He picked up his violin and left the room.

Chapter 8

Honey Doesn't Want to Be Your Friend

"What's wrong with Honey?" Kavya's screech sounded like a fire alarm. Rohan raced to his room from his parents' bedroom, where he'd been practicing violin while Kavya had been at her dance class.

"What?" Rohan asked. Honey was still sitting in the corner of her cage, frozen like a statue. "Nothing's wrong with her," he said.

Then he looked at his floor.

"Kavya," Rohan said. "Why is there guinea pig bedding all over my floor?"

"Well, Pinky and I wanted to play with Honey," Kavya said. "And she wouldn't play."

"But that doesn't explain the mess," Rohan said.

"We thought she looked lonely," Kavya said. "So we tried to get in the cage with her."

"You *what*?" Rohan asked. "That cage isn't big enough for you!"

"Pinky fit just fine. But I only put one foot in."

"Did you hurt her?" Rohan ran to his desk. Other than trembling in the corner of her cage, Honey seemed to be okay.

"No, of course not! She made some squealing noises, and we thought they might be her happy noises. But then she just went to the corner of her cage and stopped making noises at all. So Pinky and I got out and put her back on your desk."

"I'm supposed to be making her happy. Now she's terrified!" Rohan said.

"I don't see how you were making her happy by leaving her alone," Kavya said.

"I had to practice violin, and Honey didn't like it, so I went to another room."

"I want to be Honey's friend," Kavya said.

"Then you shouldn't scare her. Besides, Honey is my responsibility, not yours."

Kavya pouted. "She's not your friend, either."

"Yes, she is," Rohan said. But he wasn't so sure.

"You're not her friend," Kavya said. "Honey needs love, and you don't even want to touch her." She hugged Pinky to her chest.

"Of course I do," Rohan said. "Watch."

He went to Honey's cage and opened the door.

He swallowed. She was a guinea pig. A friendly guinea pig.

He reached for Honey.

He stretched out his fingers. Slowly. Very slowly. In a most un-carrot-like way.

Honey looked at him with her big brown eyes. She stayed frozen like a fluffy statue.

Rohan's hand was almost there. He was going to pet her.

Suddenly, Honey made a clicking sound.

"What's she doing?" Kavya asked.

Rohan kept reaching toward Honey. He would pet her. He would.

Honey opened her mouth and showed her teeth!

"Hissssssssss!" said Honey.

"Aaaaaaah!" Rohan cried, snatching his hand back.

And then Honey ran to the other corner of her cage and froze like a statue again.

"You're scared of her?" Kavya asked.

Rohan rubbed his thumb. "No, I'm not."

Kavya glanced at the guinea pig. "It looks like Honey doesn't want to be your friend. Here, Honey. Here's someone to keep you company." She placed Pinky Pig on the outside of the cage, close to where Honey was sitting.

And with that, she left the room.

Chapter 9
Dinner and Dessert

Rohan decided he couldn't spend all his time worrying about making Honey happy. He had other work to do, too. He should practice the recorder.

But Honey didn't like the violin. He wasn't sure she'd like the recorder, either.

Rohan took out his notebook and reread all the notes he'd taken about Honey when he spoke with Mrs. Z. He looked at all the doodles he'd made of her in class.

When Honey was happy, she hopped around and made squeaking noises. She didn't freeze like a statue.

"Rohan! Kavya! Time for dinner," Dad called upstairs.

That's it! Mrs. Z mentioned that Honey could have a strawberry once a week as a treat, and she hadn't had one this week.

"Hang on, Honey," Rohan said. "After I have dinner, I'll bring you some food. That will definitely cheer you up."

He went downstairs and found Dad, Mom, and Kavya in the kitchen.

"You ready for my famous Friday night pizza?" Dad asked. "Tonight I put on extra asparagus."

Every Friday night, Dad made pizza, and everyone tried to think of the grossest pizza toppings.

"Eww," Mom said. "I vote for squid pizza!"

"Eww," Kavya said. "I want worm pizza instead."

"Eww," Rohan said. "I want slimy ooze pizza!"

Dad looked in the oven. "Sadly, all we have is cheese and pepperoni."

"Eww!" everyone said.

As they ate pizza and salad, Mom asked, "How's it going with Honey?"

Kavya opened her mouth, but Rohan spoke up first. He needed to show his parents he could handle the responsibility.

"She's getting used to us," Rohan said. "Kavya was helpful. She put Pinky Pig next to the cage."

Kavya smiled proudly. Rohan relaxed a little.

"I'd like to give Honey some veggies and a strawberry after we finish eating," he said.

"Sure. I got everything from your list," Mom said. "Want to help me get things ready?"

"Yes," Rohan said. "It's all part of the job."

After a dessert of strawberries and vanilla ice cream, Rohan went upstairs with food for Honey.

"Look, Honey, I've got a treat for you!" Rohan called.

From his doorway, Rohan saw Honey in the middle of her cage. But as soon as he stepped into the room, she ran to the corner near Pinky Pig and froze again.

"Hey, Honey," he said. "No reason to be scared."

He dumped the vegetables into a bowl in the corner of the cage—the opposite corner from where Honey was sitting.

She started squeaking!

"That's it, Honey," Rohan said. "Have some yummy veggies."

Honey waddled over and started chomping on a lettuce leaf.

"See? It's not scary here," Rohan said. He smiled. He knew he could make Honey happy.

After a little while, he put the strawberry in the cage. "Here's dessert," he said.

Honey shuffled over to the strawberry and started nibbling right away. She made a funny little noise that sounded familiar.

Rohan stretched out his hand. He would pet her while she was happy.

But then he recognized the sound Honey was making.

Honey was purring.

Like a cat.

Rohan decided not to pet her just then.

Instead, he scooped out her droppings and threw them in the trash.

Eww, he thought, holding his nose.

Rohan went down to the kitchen early Saturday morning.

"Good morning," Mom said. "I'm surprised you're up."

Rohan yawned. "Honey woke me up with her little noises. I'm pretty sure she's hungry."

"How's it going?" Dad asked. "Do you need any help?"

Rohan gave an even bigger yawn. "Honey's doing great. I'm just taking up some veggies to give her along with her food pellets."

"You're being very responsible," Mom said. "I'm proud of you."

Rohan smiled. "I'll come down for my breakfast once I've fed her."

In his room, Honey chirruped at Rohan. "Yes, I know you're hungry," he said. He scooped Honey's food pellets into her bowl and added the veggies. She started eating right away, then made happy squeaks and zoomed around the cage.

After breakfast, the whole family came up to visit Honey in Rohan's room. Mom and Dad and Kavya all petted Honey, and Kavya even picked Honey up and cuddled her. Rohan drew sketches of them all.

"What about you, Rohan? Want to pet her?" Dad asked.

Rohan shook his head. "I'm happy sketching her."

That afternoon, after his soccer game, Rohan went to Adam's house and played video games. He was nowhere near as good as Adam, but he still had a lot of fun.

"How's it going with Honey?" Adam asked.

"Pretty good," Rohan said. "My parents say I'm being responsible, so I hope they say yes to my pet care business."

"I hope so, too. Look what I made this morning," Adam said. He brought out a huge poster board.

Rohan's
PET CARE
You can trust <u>ME</u> with your precious furry friends!

Email rohanspetcare@pfmail.com for more information

"Oh, wow, Adam, thanks," Rohan said. "This is awesome."

"No problem. And I know Ayana, Fia, Synclaire, and Sebastian are working on their own posters, and Emma is going to put out flyers at her family's ice cream store."

"Really?" Rohan asked. "That's amazing."

Adam nodded. "And Poppy is going to make lots more animal cookies for the Autumn Festival."

Rohan swallowed. All his classmates were really getting behind his business idea.

He couldn't let them down.

Chapter 10
Honey Feels at Home

Rohan came home from Adam's house and fed Honey more veggies. He held his nose and cleaned out her cage. He added a handful of paper bedding. He was doing it! He didn't have to pet Honey to take care of her.

He went to the living room to practice violin.

"Do you have to do that here?" Kavya asked, looking up from her book.

"I have to practice. If you don't like it, you can leave," Rohan said.

"I was here first," Kavya said.

Rohan kept playing. Kavya covered her ears.

Next, Rohan took out his recorder. As he raised it to his lips, Kavya ran out of the room.

The song still didn't sound right when he played it.

Rohan worked on sketches for his own pet care flyer, but he didn't like the way it was turning out. The pets in his sketches looked sad and scared. Dogs gazed at him with big, droopy eyes. Guinea pigs sat frozen in corners. Cats hissed and bared their teeth.

Saturday night was movie night. Rohan's family ordered Chinese food from their favorite restaurant.

"Are there any movies about elephants?" Rohan asked. "My friend Emma said that today is National Elephant Appreciation Day, and I'd like to learn more about our new school mascot."

"Let's see," Mom said, scrolling through the options on their TV. "Oh, look—there's a documentary about elephants. A documentary is a true story."

"That sounds great," Rohan said.

Dad and Kavya agreed. It was a cool night, and everyone got cozy under blankets on the sofa.

Rohan and his family learned that elephants live in herds and raise and defend their babies together.

"What are elephants scared of?" Kavya asked.

"Elephants are the biggest land animals in the world," Rohan said. "They're not scared of anything." He was a Curiosity Academy

Elephant, and he wasn't scared of anything either.

Then the elephants in the movie caused trouble—trampling through farms and eating crops, putting people and themselves in danger.

"What are those farmers supposed to do? No fence can keep out an elephant. And I don't want the farmers to hurt the elephants, but they can't let them stomp all over their farms, either," Rohan said.

"I don't know how they're going to solve this problem," Dad said.

As it turned out, the animal specialists in the movie knew what could stop an elephant: bees!

"No way!" Rohan said. "How can something so big be scared of something so small?"

"I'm afraid of bees, too," Kavya said.

"Everyone is afraid of something," Dad said.

"Even you?" Kavya asked.

"Even me," Dad said. "For the longest time, I was afraid to ride roller coasters. I went on one that was really scary when I was very young, and I've been terrified of them ever since."

"But you rode one with me at Galaxy World this summer," Rohan said.

"I did," Dad said. He looked at Mom. "It took me some time to work up the courage to do it. I almost asked Mom to go instead. I got through it, but I can't say I enjoyed it."

"If you were scared of riding the roller coaster, you could have told me," Rohan said.

"I know, buddy. But I wanted to support something you wanted to do. I didn't want to make you afraid by telling you *I* was afraid," Dad said.

"That wouldn't make me afraid," Rohan said. "Maybe I could have helped you not be afraid."

"Maybe it's good to share when we're afraid," Mom said.

They went back to watching the movie. Animal specialists set up beehives on fences around the farms. When the elephants heard the buzzing of the bees, they turned away from the fences and didn't trample any more crops—or people. The farms, the people, and the elephants all stayed safe. And elephants have great memories, so they continued to stay away from those places, and they told other elephants about them as well.

"Sometimes, you have to overcome fear," Mom said. "But sometimes you have to listen to fear, because it's telling you something important."

Rohan thought for a moment. He might be a little afraid of animals. But he was overcoming his fear by starting his pet care business. He didn't need to tell anyone about it.

On Sunday, Rohan woke up to gray skies and the rumble of thunder. He was ready for his last day with Honey. Taking care of a guinea pig was a lot of work!

Honey was acting like a statue again, huddling in the corner near Pinky Pig. Rohan grabbed some hay and scooped some food pellets for her. Once he put them in her cage, she squeaked and jumped around.

"This time, I'm going to eat my own breakfast before I give you your veggies, okay?" Rohan said.

Honey was too busy munching away to answer.

Rohan went downstairs, where Mom had made idlis—his favorite! They were shaped like fluffy doughnuts without holes. Everyone had some with coconut chutney and sambar.

"Everything still going well with Honey?" Mom asked.

"Yes," Rohan said in between bites.

"Great job, buddy," Dad said.

"Pinky's very proud of you," Kavya said.

Lightning flashed. Thunder boomed.

"Ooh!" Kavya. She put her hands over her ears. "That was loud!"

"It's just thunder," Rohan said. "Nothing to be scared of."

"Well, some of us are scared of thunder,

like elephants are scared of bees," Kavya said. "And other people are scared of animals."

Rohan's face got hot. "What's that supposed to mean?"

"Nothing," Kavya said. She rolled her eyes.

After he finished breakfast, Rohan put together a mix of lettuce, carrots, and peppers for Honey. Thunder continued to boom as he went upstairs.

"Look, Honey! Your favorites," he said as he entered his room.

He opened the cage and dumped in the veggies.

But Honey wasn't in the cage.

The guinea pig was gone!

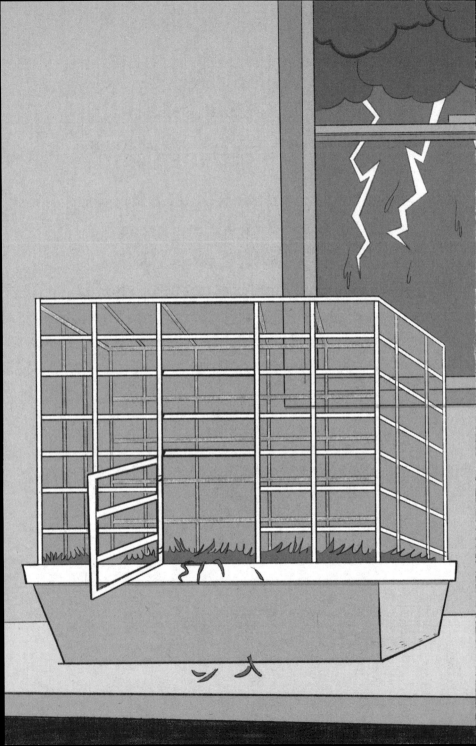

Chapter 11
Rohan Asks for Help

Where was Honey?

Rohan checked her cage again—not there! He looked on his desk. He looked on the floor and under his bed. He looked in his trash can and on his bookshelves and even in his pillowcase.

"Honey, where are you?" Rohan said.

No answer. No squeak or chirp. No sound at all.

Rohan's heart jumped around like a guinea pig hopping around its cage.

Where could Honey have gone? He had closed the cage after he'd given Honey her food pellets . . . or had he? He'd never seen her climb out of her cage at school. What had happened? He hadn't even played the violin in his room.

He couldn't lose Honey. This was the first time anyone had taken her home! What would Mrs. Z and his classmates say?

And if he was a failure at his very first pet care job, how was he going to raise money for the school garden? His friends were making posters and flyers for a business that was doomed before it even started.

Rohan put his head in his hands and took a few deep breaths. He had to make a plan— and fast!

Honey was probably somewhere on the second floor. He just had to search carefully until he found her.

Rohan went into the hallway and softly shut his bedroom door. No one was around. He snuck over to the bathroom and closed the door behind him. He looked on the floor, in the tub, in the sink. He even looked in the medicine cabinet. But Honey wasn't anywhere.

He wiped sweat off his forehead.

Rohan snuck down the hall to his parents' room. It was bigger than his room, so it took him a little longer to search. But Honey wasn't on the floor, in their closet, under their dresser, or in their bathroom.

He swallowed. A guinea pig couldn't just disappear, could it?

Finally, Rohan came to Kavya's room. Her

door was open, and she was sitting at her desk, coloring.

"Hi, Kavya," Rohan said. He looked around the floor.

"Hi! I'm making signs," Kavya said.

"Yeah? Let me see." On the way to the desk, Rohan bent to look under her bed.

"What are you doing?" Kavya asked. "I'm over here, not under the bed."

"I know." Rohan straightened up. He came over to where Kavya sat, scanning the floor for any sign of a brown-and-white guinea pig. But there wasn't even a whisker.

"What's wrong?" Kavya asked.

"Nothing?" Rohan said.

Kavya crossed her arms.

"Oh my—wow, Kavya." Rohan finally saw what his sister had been working on.

ROHANS PET CARR BIZNIS

I'M REDY TO HELP WITH YOUR PETS!

ALL MONEY WILL GO TO SCOOL GARDEN

Kavya had drawn pictures of Honey as well as dogs, cats, and a snake. And Pinky Pig. She had added a bunch of hearts and was coloring them in.

"Do you like it?" Kavya asked.

"I love it, Kavya. There's just one problem."

"What?"

Rohan sighed. "I'm not going to have a pet care business. I've lost my first customer. Honey's missing!"

Kavya gasped.

"Will you . . ." Rohan was stuck. Maybe this time, he actually needed something from his little sister. "Kavya, will you help me find her?"

Kavya stood. "You're asking me to help?"

Rohan nodded.

Kavya grinned and straightened up. "Of course I'll help. We need to think like a guinea pig. Will you try?"

"I'll try anything," Rohan said.

"Well, we know that Honey is little. And she gets scared easily. Right?"

"Right," Rohan said.

"And you put some veggies in her cage, right?"

Rohan nodded.

"Let's go back to your room."

Rohan and Kavya walked back to his room. "Shhh," Kavya whispered.

They opened the door quietly.

They tiptoed to Rohan's desk.

Something squeaked!

They got closer to Honey's cage.

Munching noises!

A brown nose was sticking into the cage.

It was Honey!

She was sitting right next to Pinky Pig, munching on a piece of lettuce!

"There you are, Honey," Kavya whispered. She carefully picked Honey up and put her back in her cage. Honey started nibbling on a carrot. She squealed.

"Thank you so much," Rohan said. "You really do know a lot about animals."

"It helps to imagine what they're feeling. Pinky and I are both scared of thunder, so I thought Honey might be, too. And I thought if she climbed out of her cage, maybe she wouldn't go far, because it's her home."

"You're right," Rohan said. "I should have thought of that."

"Well, now you can have your pet care business!"

Rohan thought for a moment. Honey was safe and sound. She had been scared, but now she wasn't.

Rohan was scared sometimes, too. Maybe he should listen to his fear.

"I think it's time to change my plan," Rohan said.

And then he started sketching.

Chapter 12
Rohan Murthy Has a New Plan

When Rohan brought Honey back to school on Monday, he talked to Mrs. Z about what had happened over the weekend.

"Thanks for telling me, Rohan," Mrs. Z said. "Would you like to go see Honey together?"

Rohan and Mrs. Z went to Honey's cage. Rohan took a baby carrot from Mrs. Z's treat bag and put it in the cage.

Honey shuffled over to the carrot and started nibbling.

Mrs. Z used a finger to gently stroke Honey's fur. "How do you feel about trying to pet her?" she asked Rohan.

Rohan nodded. He'd taken care of Honey for a whole weekend. He could do this.

He slowly moved his hand toward Honey. He reached out a finger.

Honey kept nibbling the carrot.

He touched Honey's fur. It was so soft!

Honey made a familiar noise.

"She's purring," Rohan whispered.

Mrs. Z nodded. "That means she likes you."

Rohan gave Honey one last pat, then slowly removed his hand.

"I like Honey, too." Rohan smiled. "We're both scared sometimes, but it's easier to get over being scared with a friend." Maybe that's what Dad had done when he agreed to go on the roller coaster with Rohan.

And just like Dad didn't have to keep going on rides he didn't enjoy, Rohan didn't have to keep planning a business that didn't make him happy.

After his next violin lesson, Rohan said, "I have to tell you something, Mrs. Steele."

He explained how Luna had bitten him and how that had made him afraid.

"Oh, Rohan, I'm so sorry," Mrs. Steele said. "Luna doesn't usually bite. But when she does, it's usually because she's scared. You know, people are a lot bigger than she is."

"Hmm," Rohan said. "I hadn't thought of that. But I have an idea. I'd like to sketch her for you."

Mrs. Steele smiled. "I'll hold Luna for her portrait, and you can help yourself to those cookies while you draw. Deal?"

"Deal," Rohan said.

Rohan sat at the kitchen table and picked up his pencil. He looked at Luna's yellow eyes—they were so pretty. Luna snuggled in Mrs. Steele's lap and purred.

It was a happy sound.

The weather was warm for the Autumn Festival. The sun sparkled on Lake Bluewater. Families enjoyed snacks and music. Kids laughed and rode bikes and walked their dogs.

Poppy came up to Rohan's table with a big box. "Ready, Rohan?"

"Absolutely."

She opened the box to show dozens of

sugar cookies decorated with pet faces—dogs, guinea pigs, hamsters, and cats.

"These are perfect!" Rohan said. "People are going to go wild for them."

"It was a great idea to do this together as a class," Poppy said, sitting down next to him.

They were behind a small table, and on the front was a sign:

PET PORTRAITS AND TREATS
BY MRS. Z'S THIRD GRADERS

$2 PER PORTRAIT
$2 PER COOKIE
$3 FOR BOTH!

ALL PROCEEDS TO BENEFIT
THE CURIOSITY ACADEMY
GARDEN

There was lots of glitter on the sign.

"Rohan, I have a customer for you!" Emma cried.

"Thanks, Emma," Rohan said. "I'm ready for them."

Emma and Bongo came over with Amanda and Tiny.

"This idea is so cool!" Amanda said.

"Thanks," Rohan said. "Everyone in Mrs. Z's third-grade class is helping."

"That makes it even cooler," Amanda said.

Rohan grinned. "Is Tiny ready?"

Amanda told Tiny to sit. "Yes. Go right ahead."

"Would you like a cookie while Rohan works?" Poppy asked.

Amanda chose a pug cookie and bit into it. "Delicious."

Rohan closed one eye. He looked at Tiny's

furry face. Tiny looked at Rohan and smiled a dog smile.

After a few minutes, Rohan turned to Amanda. "Done. What do you think?"

"It's perfect," Amanda said. "Thanks so much. Here you go." She handed Emma three dollars, and Emma put them in a box.

Rohan gave Amanda the drawing.

"Look at this," Emma said to Amanda. She showed her the sketch of Bongo that Rohan had made. "I'm going to put this up in my locker at school."

Rohan, Poppy, and their classmates were very busy all morning.

Once he'd done a quick sketch of a happy corgi and Poppy had sold the owner a hamster cookie, Rohan asked Steven how much they had made.

Steven counted the bills in the box. "Twenty-seven dollars so far," he said.

Adam stopped by. "More customers are coming soon. Do you two need a break?"

"I'm fine," Poppy said.

"I'm not tired at all," Rohan said. "I'm having a great time!"

"We all are," Ayana said.

"I'm glad I changed my plan," Rohan said. "I'm not really someone who likes to pet animals. But I really love to draw them."

"Now we all get to help the school garden," Carlota said.

"Sometimes we have to change plans when we have more information," Mom said. She had come to the table with Dad and Kavya. "That's an important part of business and life."

"It's also important to ask for help when you need it," Rohan said, grinning at his sister.

Kavya grinned back.

Ruthie came up to the table with a cat carrier. "Hey, Rohan, will you sketch my friend's new kitten?"

"Absolutely," Rohan said. "Cats are great." He laughed. "Especially from sketching distance."

© Carter Hasegawa

About the Author

RAJANI LaROCCA was born in India, raised in Kentucky, and now lives in eastern Massachusetts, where she practices medicine and writes award-winning books for young readers, including the Newbery Honor–winning *Red, White, and Whole*.

Rajani's favorite third-grade memory is a science experiment where her class grew pea plants, then observed aphids, crickets, and a chameleon as they ate the pea plants (and each other). It was one of the experiences that inspired her to study science and eventually become a doctor (for people).

rajanilarocca.com

About the Illustrator

KAT FAJARDO (they/she) received a Pura Belpré Honor for Illustration for their first graphic novel, *Miss Quinces* (published in Spanish as *Srta. Quinces*). Born and raised in New York City, Kat now lives in Austin, Texas, with their pups, Mac and Roni.

katfajardo.com

The Creators of
The Kids in Mrs. Z's Class

William Alexander

Kyle Lukoff

Tracey Baptiste

Kekla Magoon

Martha Brockenbrough

Meg Medina

Lamar Giles

Kate Messner

Karina Yan Glaser

Olugbemisola Rhuday-Perkovich

Mike Jung

Eliot Schrefer

Hena Khan

Laurel Snyder

Rajani LaRocca

Linda Urban

Read on for a preview of Book Three in the series,

Poppy Song Bakes a Way

BY **KARINA YAN GLASER**

"There you are!" Olive said, her fabric lunch bag unopened on the table in front of her. She was finger knitting with purple sparkly yarn. By the time Poppy sat down, Olive had ended the knit rope she was making and tied the ends together. Then she put the knitted necklace around Poppy's head.

"Voilà!" Olive said. "That's a fancy French way of saying, 'Here you go!' We were waiting for you before we started to eat. Well, except for Rohan." She glared at him.

Rohan froze, his sandwich already half gone. "Sorry! I couldn't wait," he said, his mouth full. "My stomach was telling me it needed something in it, fast!"

Poppy laughed as she opened her lunch box and spread her three food trays on the table.

"Ooh," Synclaire said, looking over. "What's in your lunch today?"

"My grandma and I made mini pineapple buns yesterday. She put a bunch in my lunch box to share with you," Poppy said. "Do you want some?"

Of course everyone wanted one. Olive made grabby hands as Poppy passed the tray around.

"These buns are delicious," Olive said to Poppy.

Sebastian touched a napkin to the side of his mouth. "Please tell your grandmother she is a superb baker."

"You can tell her yourself!" Poppy said. "She's coming to school next week for Valued Visitor Day!"

"Hooray!" said Rohan. "My mom loved being the Valued Visitor."

"Will she bring more of these pineapple buns?" Olive asked.

"Actually," Poppy said, "on the day she comes, it will be her birthday! So I thought *I* should make something for *her*!"

"Ooh, what are you going to make?" Synclaire asked.

Poppy thought about her conversation with Memo. Po Po had been teaching Poppy so much about baking. If Poppy could make Dragon's Beard candy all by herself, then Po Po would know she had taught Poppy well. It would be the best birthday present.

"Dragon's Beard candy," Poppy said with conviction. "It's made from very thin strands of sugar, sort of like cotton candy."

Olive, Rohan, Sebastian, and Synclaire cheered. Emma, who was sitting at the table next to theirs, asked, "Why's everyone so happy?"

Olive gave her an update, and word spread

throughout the lunchroom within minutes. By the time they got in line to return to their classroom, *everyone* in Mrs. Z's class knew about the Dragon's Beard candy. And everyone was excited!

Poppy was excited . . . and nervous. Po Po was her favorite person, and she knew her whole class would love her. They would have a huge birthday celebration. All Poppy needed to do was figure out how to make Dragon's Beard candy and keep it a surprise from Po Po until the big day.